YOU CAN DO IT!

by Betsy Lewin

I
Like to
Read®

Holiday House / New York

For Ted,
who always could

I LIKE TO READ is a registered trademark of Holiday House, Inc.

Copyright © 2013 by Betsy Lewin
All Rights Reserved
HOLIDAY HOUSE is registered in the U.S. Patent and Trademark Office.
Printed and Bound in October 2012 at Tien Wah Press, Johor Bahru, Johor, Malaysia.
The text typeface is Report School Regular.
The artwork was created with pen and ink line and watercolor washes.
www.holidayhouse.com
First Edition
1 3 5 7 9 10 8 6 4 2

Library of Congress Cataloging-in-Publication Data
Lewin, Betsy.
You can do it! / by Betsy Lewin. — 1st ed.
p. cm. — (I like to read)
Summary: Two alligators challenge each other and themselves
as they compete in a race.
ISBN 978-0-8234-2522-8 (hardcover)
[1. Self-confidence—Fiction. 2. Racing—Fiction.
3. Alligators—Fiction.] I. Title.
PZ7.L58417You 2013
[E]—dc23
2011051992

I Like to Read® Books
You will like all of them!

Paperback and Hardcover

Boy, Bird, and Dog by David McPhail

Dinosaurs Don't, Dinosaurs Do by Steve Björkman

The Lion and the Mice
by Rebecca Emberley and Ed Emberley

See Me Run by Paul Meisel
A Theodor Seuss Geisel Award Honor Book

Hardcover

Car Goes Far by Michael Garland

Fish Had a Wish by Michael Garland

The Fly Flew In by David Catrow

I Have a Garden by Bob Barner

I Will Try by Marilyn Janovitz

Late Nate in a Race by Emily Arnold McCully

Look! by Ted Lewin

Mice on Ice by Rebecca Emberley
and Ed Emberley

Pig Has a Plan by Ethan Long

Sam and the Big Kids by Emily Arnold McCully

See Me Dig by Paul Meisel

Sick Day by David McPhail

You Can Do It! by Betsy Lewin

Visit holidayhouse.com to read more
about I Like to Read® Books.